MALKE'S SECRET RECIPE
A Chanukah Story

David A. Adler
illustrated by Joan Halpern

KAR-BEN COPIES, INC.   ROCKVILLE, MD

Library of Congress Cataloging-in-Publication Data

Adler, David A.
  Malke's secret recipe.

  Bibliography: p.
  Summary: In the foolish town of Chelm, Berel the shoemaker attempts to duplicate the secret
recipe of Malke's potato pancakes, but his wife's interference makes his plan go awry.
  [1. Jews—Fiction. 2. Cookery—Fiction] I. Halpern, Joan, ill. II. Title.
PZ7.A2615Mal 1989   [E]   88-32019
ISBN 0-9340494-88-1
ISBN 0-9340494-89-X (pbk.)

Published by KAR-BEN COPIES, INC., Rockville, MD   1-800-4-KARBEN
Printed in the United States of America

MALKE'S SECRET RECIPE
A Chanukah Story

Chelm

There are two Chelms. One is a real city in Poland, where Jews have lived for hundreds of years. The other is the city of "wise men" which exists in Jewish folklore.

According to legend, after God created the universe, He sent off an angel carrying two sacks filled with souls. One sack held souls of the wise; the other sack held souls of the foolish. As the angel soared over the earth, he distributed the souls, half and half, so that no community might have too many of one kind. Just as he reached Chelm, one of his sacks caught on the tip of a hill. It ripped open and spilled all of its foolish souls into the one tiny town.

Some believe that the people of Chelm were really wise; they just happened to do many foolish things. And of course the foolishness did not stop on Chanukah. The people of Chelm were wise men—or fools—every day of the year.

In Chelm, as in other towns, each family had its own latke recipe. In some families the recipe had been handed down from mother to daughter for many generations. Some people added just salt and pepper to the potatoes. Others added eggs and onions. There were even people who added paprika, parsley, and bread crumbs.

Most people were happy to share their latke recipes. But not Malke, the tailor's wife.

"I may be a poor woman," Malke said, "but I make the best latkes in Chelm, and I'm the only one who has the recipe."

When Malke was a young bride, she would let people taste her latkes. She wanted everyone to know how good they were. But Malke became afraid that someone eating her latkes might be able to taste each ingredient and learn her recipe. Since then, she only let her husband and children eat her famous latkes.

As the years passed, Malke's latkes tasted
even better in people's memories than they
had tasted on their forks.

Berel, the shoemaker, always closed his eyes
and smiled when he remembered Malke's
latkes. "They were so very soft," he would tell
his wife Yentel, "and so very light. Eating
Malke's latkes was like eating a cloud."

Then one Chanukah night, Berel, Yentel, and their children were eating latkes. These were not soft and light latkes, but thick, heavy ones.

Berel took one bite and banged on the table. "Enough!" he shouted. "I'm tired of the same latkes every Chanukah. Tomorrow I'm getting Malke's recipe."

The next morning Berel told Yentel, "I'm
not opening the shop today. If someone
comes with his shoes, tell him to come back
tomorrow. But don't tell him where I've gone."

Berel hid behind a tree near Malke's house.
He waited there all day, but Malke didn't
make latkes.

That night, Berel watched as Malke and her family lit their Chanukah candles. He heard them sing *Maoz Tzur*, "Rock of Ages," and he watched them play dreidel.

Then Berel saw Malke take out some
potatoes, a grater, and a large pan.

"This is it!" Berel said to himself. "Tonight I will eat latkes as soft and light as a cloud."

Berel crawled close to the window. He watched and wrote down everything Malke did.

When the latkes were done, Berel ran home to his wife Yentel.

"I've got it!" he said. "I've got Malke's recipe."

Berel looked at his paper. "First take five
potatoes and two eggs," he read.

"Some secret recipe," Yentel said as she
watched Berel peel the potatoes. "We always
use potatoes and eggs."

Berel grated the potatoes into a bowl. He added the eggs.

"We do that, too," Yentel said.

"Now," Berel read. "Chop six scallions very fine."

"Scallions!" Yentel said. "Who ever heard of using scallions in latkes? Everyone uses an onion. An onion is better."

"So I'll use an onion," Berel said. He chopped it and mixed it in with the potatoes.

"Next," Berel said, "Malke mixed in flour."

"Don't use flour. Use bread crumbs," Yentel said.

Berel used bread crumbs.

Berel added some salt. He looked down at his paper and was about to add pepper when Yentel shook her head and said, "Pepper makes me sneeze."

Berel didn't add the pepper.

"Now I need a lemon," Berel said. "Malke squeezed in a few drops of lemon juice."

Yentel shook her head. "No. Lemon juice belongs in tea."

"And Malke added parsley," Berel continued. "She made her latkes very thin and fried them in vegetable oil."

"Parsley! Vegetable oil! That's not a secret recipe. That's secret nonsense," Yentel said. Parsley belongs in a salad with carrots. In this house we fry in chicken fat. And thick latkes taste better than thin ones."

Berel and Yentel made their latkes with potatoes, eggs, salt, and breadcrumbs, just like they always did. They made their latkes very thick and fried them in chicken fat.

When the latkes were done, Berel and Yentel and their children sat down to eat them. They ate slowly. They wanted to know if Malke's latkes really did taste better than anyone else's.

"These latkes don't taste soft and light," one of the children said.

"And they don't taste like clouds," another added.

"Some secret recipe," Berel told Yentel after all the latkes were eaten. "They taste just like ours."

"Well," Yentel said, "this just proves that no matter how you make them, latkes always taste the same."

CHANUKAH

More than 2,000 years ago, a Syrian king, Antiochus IV, ruled over Israel. He tried to force Jews to worship Greek idols and follow Greek traditions. Many refused. A small band of Jews, the Maccabees, fought the mighty armies of Antiochus and won. When the Maccabees returned to restore their Holy Temple in Jerusalem, they found only one small jar of pure oil, enough to keep the Temple menorah burning for just one day. But a miracle happened, and the oil burned and burned for eight days and nights.

Today, Jews all over the world celebrate Chanukah to recall the Maccabees' victory. They light candles for eight nights and share potato latkes (pancakes) fried in oil, to remind them of the Chanukah miracle.

MALKE'S SECRET RECIPE

5 potatoes (you can leave peels on)
6 scallions
3 TBSP flour
2 eggs
1 tsp. salt (more to taste)
¼ tsp. pepper
1 tsp. lemon juice
1 tsp. parsley flakes
Vegetable oil for frying

Scrub potatoes and grate or shred in food processor. Add rest of ingredients and process until just mixed. Heat oil in large skillet. Carefully drop latkes by large spoonfuls into hot oil and brown on both sides.* Drain on paper towels and serve immediately with apple sauce or sour cream.

* Hot oil can be dangerous. Make sure an adult is helping you.

ABOUT THE AUTHOR

David A. Adler is the author of more than 80 fiction and nonfiction works for young readers, including the Cam Jansen Mysteries, several biographies, and two titles on the Kar-Ben list, *The House on the Roof* and *Jewish Holiday Fun*. His book, *The Number on My Grandfather's Arm,* won the Sydney Taylor Book Award of the Association of Jewish Libraries. Mr. Adler is a Senior Editor of the Jewish Publication Society and lives with his wife and family in New York.

ABOUT THE ILLUSTRATOR

Joan Halpern has been active in the field of design and advertising for 25 years. A graduate of The Parsons School of Design, she headed catalog production and creative services for Childcraft Education Corporation, and has done extensive work for the New Jersey State Council for the Arts. Her illustrations for *The Carp in the Bathtub* and *Not Yet, Elijah!* (Kar-Ben) have been widely acclaimed. This is her fourth book.